FROM THE

☐ hum

☐ ho-hum

LIBRARY OF

....

THE

ADVENTURES OF

Miss Petitfour

ANNE MICHAELS

with illustrations by

EMMA BLOCK

BLOOMSBURY
LONDON OXFORD NEW YORK NEW DELHI SYDNEY

Bloomsbury Publishing, London, Oxford, New York, New Delhi and Sydney

First published in Great Britain in November 2015 by Bloomsbury Publishing Plc
50 Bedford Square, London WC1B 3DP

First published in Canada by Tundra Books,
a division of Random House of Canada Limited,
a Penguin Random House Company

This paperback edition published April 2017

www.bloomsbury.com

BLOOMSBURY is a registered trademark of Bloomsbury Publishing Plc

Text copyright © Anne Michaels 2015
Illustrations copyright © Emma Block 2015

The moral rights of the author and illustrator have been asserted

A CIP catalogue record for this book is available from the British Library

ISBN 978 1 4088 6805 8

FSC
MIX
Paper
FSC® C020056

Printed and bound in China by Leo Paper Products, Heshan, Guangdong

1 3 5 7 9 10 8 6 4 2

For R and E

CONTENTS

Introducing

Miss Petitfour

Very soon you will be meeting Miss Petitfour,
and so, just to be sure you'll recognise her,
this is what she looks like.

. . . *and her*

Cats

Minky, the littlest cat, looks as if she stepped in snow when she was a kitten and the snow never melted. She is all black except for her white paws and the spots on her head and tail, where the snow didn't melt either.

Misty is the colour of rain on a window.

Taffy is the colour of toast and butter.

Purrsia is silver, long-haired and likes to nap on magazines.

Pirate looks as if he just rubbed the sleep from his eyes and left behind two little smudges of orange. Elsewhere, he has patches of black and white.

Mustard is the yellow of . . . mustard, and he has a grey moustache.

Moutarde is the yellow of . . . Dijon mustard, and he wears a beret.

Hemdela is black with a white shirt front. She likes soup.

Earring is a Siamese
who loves shiny things.

Grigorovitch is chocolate-brown,
and the tip of his tail looks like it
has been tasting vanilla icing off
the top of a cake (which tells you
something about him).

Clasby wears a bobble hat,
knitted for him for
his fifth birthday.
He loves to draw
and paint.

Of all the captains, Captain Captain
is the oldest and wisest. He has many
stories to tell from the days when he was
a ship's cat. He is a blue-grey British
shorthair with a lovely round, bearded
face. Sometimes he wears his captain's hat.

Captain Captain's son, Captain Catkin, is a bit mischievous and is grey and white like a winter sea.

Captain Clothespin is Captain Captain's daughter and Captain Catkin's sister. She loves to dance and is silver and white like a skating rink in moonlight.

Your Shyness believes she is descended from royalty. She wears a lace collar and has silky fur, bright as a gold coin.

Sizzles is a ginger cat. He is little but very long.

MISS PETITFOUR
and the
RATTLING
SPOON

S ome adventures are so small, you hardly know they've happened. Like the adventure of sharpening your pencil to a perfect point, just before it breaks and that little bit gets stuck in the sharpener. That, I think we will all agree, is a very small adventure.

Other adventures are so big and last so long, you might forget they are adventures at all – like growing up.

And some adventures are just the right size – fitting into a single, magical day. And these are the sorts of adventures Miss Petitfour had.

No one knew where Miss Petitfour got her name. Did an ancient Petitfour invent those fancy iced cakes called *petit fours* (which conveniently rhymes with *spaghetti store*)? You know, those miniature cakes that disappear in one bite, cakes so small you don't have to share? Was it because one of her great-great-great-grandfathers was such a splendid baker of little cakes, or was it because he was simply so very good at eating them? Miss Petitfour herself was an expert at both.

If Miss Petitfour were short, and if she were a bird, you might say she was as prim and proud as a sparrow. But Miss Petitfour was not short – she was tall – and so you'd have to say she was as spindly as a stork. Her legs were as thin as string with two knots for her knees and two knots for her ankles. And, just as one might expect of someone who likes to fly, she had billowy hair that she wore all brushed up in a tumbling bun. The more she brushed up, the more it came down, and misty wisps floated about her head. She liked to wear a woollen coat that flounced when she walked and jingled with a row of silver buttons. Almost everything she wore (except her shoes) ended in zigzagging scallops of lace and rickrack. She was especially fond of pockets, paisley, playful patterns and anything hand-knitted.

On windy days, Miss Petitfour always took her cats out for an airing. There was Minky, Misty, Taffy, Purrsia, Pirate, Mustard, Moutarde, Hemdela, Earring, Grigorovitch, Clasby, Captain Captain, Captain Catkin, Captain Clothespin, Your Shyness and Sizzles. The cats liked to be aired. They liked to feel the wind pick up every one of their hairs and set them down again, gently, as if the wind were looking for something.

In one hand, Miss Petitfour would hold the littlest cat, Minky, and with the other she would choose her favourite tea-party tablecloth, bringing together the four corners in her fist and straightening her arm into the wind. Immediately, the tablecloth would puff up like a biscuit in the oven, and swiftly

Miss Petitfour's shiny shoes would lift from the earth. Then, one by one, Minky, Misty, Taffy, Purrsia, Pirate, Mustard, Moutarde, Hemdela, Earring, Grigorovitch, Clasby, Captain Captain, Captain Catkin, Captain Clothespin and Your Shyness, with little-but-long Sizzles at the end, lifted off with Miss Petitfour, each cat with its tail wrapped to another.

How the cats loved their flights with Miss Petitfour!

The cats swung down like a strand of wool or a skipping rope or a loose hair ribbon, sixteen cats dangling in one gigantic puss-tail. Then, when Miss Petitfour spotted her destination below – the bakery or the bookshop or The-Cream-and-Cream-Bun Cafe (the cats' favourite) – she neatly shortened sail and drifted down, landing tidily on her toes, followed by dozens of dainty little paws as the waterfall of cats poured and purred into the street. The cats had to be careful of their tails when landing, so as not to get tangled in trees and clotheslines and gargoyles and other such obstacles.

Everyone in the village was used to Miss Petitfour's mode of travel, and no one blinked an eye except to say hello.

Miss Petitfour always travelled by tablecloth, that is to say, by air. First, she would take a measure of the *meteorological circumstances*, that is to say, the weather. Then she would position herself accordingly, only attempting errands that were *propitious*, that is to say, favourable. In short, she would fly in whatever direction the wind blew her. If the wind were blowing eastward, for example, she would go to the pet shop (to browse for the latest in cat toys), and to Mr Patel's Bakery (for treats with icing, whipped cream or crunchy crusts), and to Mrs Carruther's Grocery Shop (where the avocado pears were always exactly right, neither too hard nor too *quaggy*, that is to say, squeezy). But if the wind were westerly, she would take advantage of that fact and do her banking, then visit the bookshop, the zoo, Mr Clemmo's Hardware Shop, or take something in for repair to Mr Pomeroy, who could fix anything that had springs in it – a watch, a wind-up toy, a mechanical hat. (Mr Pomeroy loved springs, ever since he was a boy, and so he made them his life's work. 'What use is a job if it doesn't have springs in it?' he would say, and of course he was perfectly right.)

Miss Petitfour did not live far from the village – just a short flight – and she always liked to hover above and admire the view. Every shop had a big wooden sign that swung and creaked in the breeze. And every sign was in the shape of what was sold in the shop. So, for example, the sign for Mr Patel's Bakery was in the shape of a great wooden cupcake, and the sign for Mrs Collarwaller's Bookshop was a giant book, and the sign for Mr Clemmo's Hardware Shop was a gigantic hammer. In this way, the village was friendly to everyone, even to the youngest who didn't yet know how to read, or to a stranger who spoke a foreign language; everyone would know which shop was which, and no one would go into the bakery expecting to buy a pair of shoes.

Mrs Collarwaller, the bookseller, was a particular friend of Miss Petitfour, and the bookshop was one

of Miss Petitfour's favourite places. There were two sides to Mrs Collarwaller's shop: one side for adventure books and the other for books in which nothing ever happens. Mrs Collarwaller preferred books where nothing ever happens, but even she understood that sometimes we feel the need to visit another planet, or to run away to sea to meet pirates, or to fall down holes, or to be blasted by a volcano, and that sort of thing. So, one side of the shop was the ho-hum and the other was the hum, although which was which depended on what sort of book the customer liked best.

Mrs Collarwaller herself mostly liked books where people sat knitting by the fire with a plate of biscuits and a mug of steaming cocoa beside them, dreaming about the day Lord Somersault or Lady Hopscotch would come to tea, with detailed descriptions of all they would eat: buttery shortbread that greases your fingers, jam doughnuts oozing fruit, eclairs dipped in chocolate and full of air. Not to mention crisp Florentines, fluffy Neapolitans and custardy custard squares. Mrs Collarwaller loved books in which people talked a lot and thought aloud, had dreams, discussed recipes and looked at each other with affection. She liked books full of interesting facts that would never come in useful and were therefore always the most fascinating sort of facts to know. For example, the kind of food ostriches like best, or the history of doilies, or all the movies in which the Isetta bubble car appears, or important details concerning the invention of shoelaces. And, it bears repeating, anything involving doilies.

Wise Mrs Collarwaller was convinced that if you knew these sorts of things, you were more likely to bump up against occasions when such information was needed, just as if you had an ice-cream machine in your kitchen, you were far more likely to eat ice

cream than not. But then there were others who believed that having an ice-cream machine meant exactly the opposite, that one would tire of home-made chocolate marshmallow ribbon and therefore rarely eat it at all, and of course this discussion was just the sort of thing Mrs Collarwaller liked to read about and would be in a book one would find in the ho-hum – or was it the hum? – half of her bookshop.

People often say that children have no use for long words, but frankly, Mrs Collarwaller found this never to be the case. In her vast experience, children loved books that contained words such as *propitious*, *perambulator* and *gesticulate*, especially if they all ended up in the same sentence. The kind of word your tongue could get tangled up and lost in. She was very helpful to her young customers, suggesting, for example, that if they wished to finish reading a particular book before they fell asleep, then they'd better start reading while still in the bathtub; that way, they'd be on page thirty-three by the time they were pulling their arms into their pyjama sleeves, and more than halfway by the time their head was on the pillow. Mrs Collarwaller had many good ideas, such as printing an entire story on one's pillowcase, so that there would always be something to read if one woke in the middle of the night. (Of course, like all the best booksellers, she kept a fresh supply of flashlights and batteries by the cash register, for those who like to read under the blankets.)

Miss Petitfour and Mrs Collarwaller spent many enjoyable hours drinking tea together in the bookshop and playing a game they were both extremely fond of: thinking up titles for books too silly ever to be written, such as BEWARE, I'M GOING TO ROB YOU ANY MINUTE, or WARNING: THE LAST PAGE IS MISSING, or THIS BOOK IS A WASTE OF TIME, or HOW TO CARE FOR THE FISH IN YOUR SHOE, or DON'T BOTHER, ALL THE PAGES ARE STUCK TOGETHER, or I THINK I'M ASLEEP.

Do you know what a *digression* is? Well, of course you do. A *digression* is like quicksand or a whirlpool – sometimes you just can't find your way out of one. It's the part of a story that some people think is the most fun, when the story wanders off the point and gets lost, giving us all sorts of information that has nothing to do with getting us from the beginning to the end. A *digression* is just like what happens when you're walking to school: you stop to tie your shoelaces and notice the neighbour's dog looking at you, and so you stop to give it a pat, and then you see the fence has started to fall down, and so you have to climb it just a little, and then you look up and realise the clouds are in the shape of pianos, and then, oh dear, you suddenly remember you were on your way to school and you have to run all the rest of the way so you won't be late. *That* is a *digression*.

Now, where were we?

Miss Petitfour's sixteen cats were very fond of arts and crafts. They especially loved to make elaborate costumes for themselves and to decorate absolutely everything. And so, off they would go, with Miss Petitfour, through the air to the Sew-a-Lot Shop (the shop's sign was a big spool of thread), where they collected ribbons and shimmery satin,

delicate lace and knubbly wool, small panels of crêpe paper, squares of felt, bolts of plush velvet, bushels of buttons and reams of silver foil. Then they would return home to sew, knit, cut, paste, tie, scrunch, fold, drape, tape, crochet, embroider and generally decorate away.

The cats decorated each other and then displayed themselves in dramatic poses on the carpet, or dripping from the arms of Miss Petitfour's over-stuffed chairs. Sometimes they even decorated Miss Petitfour, adorning her with feathers or fabric.

The puss-cats were also fond of making them-selves into sculptures – swirly structures that were just for show. They liked to pretend they were fancy staircases, balconies, wrought-iron banisters, baskets and chandeliers, and they often needed a tail detangler to sort themselves out afterwards.

And when they were finally tired out from all their artistic activity, they would fall asleep in the hammock in the back garden, dreaming of buns sodden with freshly whipped cream and vats of dipping chocolate. Or sometimes they joined

Miss Petitfour for a nap on the sunny porch, where they would lie in a lovely mound of cosy and tangled cat-spaghetti, with a hum – or a ho-hum – book open across Miss Petitfour's lap.

Sometimes stories will have three special words right in the middle of them, like three shiny buttons down a shirt front or a dress, or three shiny screws in a shiny hinge. These three little words, 'THEN ONE DAY', open a story like a tiny key. (Words are often keys, as your parents have no doubt told you, and open things very nicely – *please*, *thank you*, *yes*, *no*, *may I*.) So now, before the 'ho' creeps forever ahead of the 'hum', let us use those three little words.

THEN ONE DAY, as Miss Petitfour was setting the table for tea, she noticed the empty marmalade pot, with the spoon still in it. Could it be true? She rattled the silver spoon in the empty jar. (And rattled it again because she liked the sound it made.) Well, this was surely one of the most unheard-of things she had ever heard of. Teatime without marmalade? It was unthinkable (though she had just

thought it). It was the most unthinkable thought she had ever thought. Without a moment to lose, Miss Petitfour chose a table-cloth and called her cats around her and rushed into the garden for lift-off.

Miss Petitfour was very particular about which tablecloths she chose for her flights with the cats. A sunny day called for a starched white cloth, so she would seem to be floating gracefully from a cloud. A rainy day called for a transparent plastic tablecloth, as invisible as the rain itself. And in autumn, when the sky was a deep shade of plum or grey, Miss Petitfour brought out her brightest, most colourful cloth, so that the reds, oranges and golds would glow against the dark sky, and anyone looking up would think that the top of a beautiful autumn tree had lifted from its trunk and was floating away.

And today, because they were simply off to the shops, Miss Petitfour had her trusty paisley cloth in hand. Paisley was Miss Petitfour's choice for everyday jolly good fun, just because she liked the swirls and curls so much.

Unfortunately, however, the wind was blowing in the direction of the bank and not in the direction of Mrs Carruther's Grocery Shop. Miss Petitfour stood for a moment, thinking what to do. (It is often the case that the wind is not blowing in the right direction. This is just another tiresome fact of life, like the fact that your feet grow too big for your favourite shoes, or that your favourite crayon gets shorter and shorter the more you use it.) Perhaps, thought Miss Petitfour, she could ride the wind the wrong way and circle around the whole globe to Mrs Carruther's shop . . . Well, do you think this is wise? To go the wrong way to get somewhere? The more Miss Petitfour thought about it, the more she liked the idea, for she liked circles, and anything made in the shape of a circle – doughnuts, biscuits, pancakes – so she straightened her arm to the wind and off they flew.

It was very gusty, but definitely not a wind for marmalade; it was a wind for Mr Clemmo's Hardware

Shop, a wind for buying doorknobs and sandpaper squares and for the distinctive hardware shop smell of nails and paint. It was a wind for eyeglasses, pinch-purses, stationery, paper clips, footballs and car repair. But it was most definitely not a wind for buying marmalade.

The last cat on the line, the slender ginger named Sizzles, wasn't so keen on circular things; he liked things that went one way at a time, long things he could eat one end to another, not things that always took you back to where you started. He liked sausages, french fries, linguine and liquorice ropes. Little-but-long Sizzles did not approve of going the wrong way to get to where you want to go.

So, as they passed the town hall, Sizzles stretched as far as he could and boldly captured the top of the clock tower, wrapping his tail around it. Miss Petitfour and all her cats suddenly twanged to a stop, mid-air. And there they quavered, suspended in the high wind, sixteen tails taut as a wire, stiff as a clothesline, across the town.

Sizzles had stopped the flight!

The wind was now quite a bit more than a gusty gust, and the line of cats, stiff as a cable, stood out against the white sky like a fuzzy streak of black marker on a white piece of paper.

MEANWHILE (another word that opens stories like a key), below, Mrs Carruther, who happened to be sweeping the pavement outside her grocery shop, looked up. She looked up because her sweet son Carlos Cornelius Carruther, sitting in his *perambulator*, had let out a shrill gurgle and was

pointing eagerly – one might say, *gesticulating* – to the cats in the sky. The giggling baby looked proud, as babies often do. (Babies like to feel proud.)

Mrs Carruther took up her binoculars, which always hung by a red ribbon around her neck (she was an avid bird-watcher), and focused them on the strange arrangement in the sky. And she saw Miss Petitfour hovering above the town hall, about a block away, mouthing the word 'marmalade'.

Generous Mrs Carruther understood the difficulty at once. She hurried into her shop and, without a thought to the expense, snatched a pot of Thick-Cut Orange Marmalade from a shelf. She ran with her baby in the *perambulator* to the town hall, climbed to the roof and, bravely clinging to the shingles, held out the pot. Immediately it was seized by Sizzles and passed from paw to paw, from Sizzles to Your Shyness to Captain Clothespin to Captain Catkin to Captain Captain to Clasby to Grigorovitch to Earring to Hemdela to Moutarde to Mustard to Pirate to Purrsia to Taffy to Misty to Minky, who plopped it into Miss Petitfour's basket.

In order to seize the pot of marmalade, however, Sizzles had to unwind his tail from the roof, and at that very same instant of snapping up the marmalade, off the cats had shot, like an arrow on the roaring wind, while they madly passed the jar up the line.

The flight was on!

Now, at the very edge of the village, towards which Miss Petitfour and the cats were racing at high speed, a little red sports car, with the top down, happened to be waiting at a traffic light. Who was it but the *debonair*, that is to say, charming (and really very shy) Mr Coneybeare, the owner of Coneybeare's Confetti, the king of confetti himself. Mr Coneybeare was rather fond of Miss Petitfour and was far too timid to tell her so. In fact, at that very moment, waiting for the traffic light to change, he had been daydreaming, trying to think of ways he might earn her friendship.

Now, it must be made very clear that it was not the case that Mr Coneybeare had been aimlessly driving round the village hoping to catch a glimpse of Miss Petitfour, but truly and absolutely a wild coincidence that, JUST THEN, at the very moment he was waiting at the traffic light, there blew another particularly gusty gust that was just about to carry Miss Petitfour and her cats all the way around the world in the wrong direction. And it also must be said that, now that they had their marmalade, hungry Sizzles was more determined than ever to get home to his tea and not go the wrong way around to get there. And so, Sizzles, the last cat on the line, catching sight of his chance, cleverly – and just in time – tucked his tail around Mr Coneybeare's steering wheel and, with one quick tail action, captured the car! Of course, Mr Coneybeare was delighted to be of service. With Sizzles' tail curled neatly around Mr Coneybeare's steering wheel, Miss Petitfour and the cats hitched a ride against the wind, back to Miss Petitfour's cottage, singing gleefully all the way – 'Hullaba-one, hullaba-two, hullaba-loo, hullaba-MEW!'

Down the road they sped, Miss Petitfour and her tablecloth like a paisley balloon, attached to the little red sports car by a furry string.

Miss Petitfour believed firmly that every adventure past her doorstep – even just a jaunt to the grocery shop – must end with a tea party, and the dashing Mr Coneybeare was invited. In the middle of the table, in a silver bowl, was placed the precious marmalade, which glowed like gold in its shining dish. Before Minky, Misty, Taffy, Purrsia, Mustard, Moutarde, Hemdela, Earring, Clasby and Your Shyness, who all loved round things, Miss Petitfour placed huge bowls of frothed milk. And before Pirate, Grigorovitch, Captain Captain, Captain Catkin, Captain Clothespin and Sizzles, who all liked long things, she placed especially lengthy chocolate eclairs crammed with whipped cream, which they gobbled up with great cat smiles from the beginning to THE END.

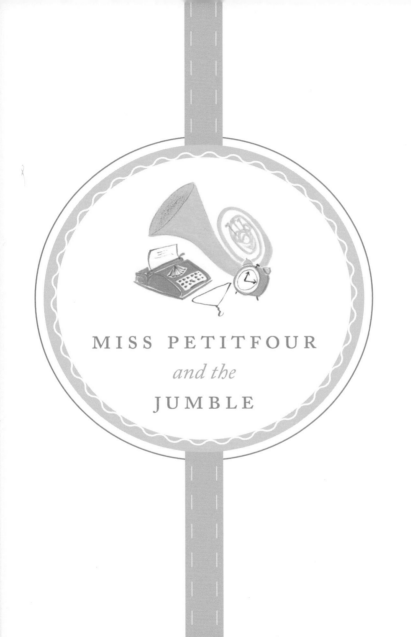

MISS PETITFOUR
and the
JUMBLE

It was a lovely spring day, with the taste of liquorice on the breeze, and little green shoots shooting all about, and tender tendrils all alive with leaf, and Miss Petitfour decided it was time to give her wee cottage a proper clean-out.

Sometimes, opening one's closet is as much of an adventure as an expedition into the wilderness. Especially in the spring, and especially Miss Petitfour's closet, because all winter every bit of string, every particularly attractive sweet wrapper, every yo-yo with chipped paint, every sock with a hole in the toe, every unusually bumpy rock found in the playground, every twig shaped like a *Y*, every bent colander, every tweezer that no longer tweezes, every broken gizmo was thrown in, and the closet door quickly slammed behind it.

To assist her in her spring cleaning, Miss Petitfour asked her young friend Pleasant Patel, the baker's daughter who lived with her family above Mr Patel's Bakery, to come and open the closet with her. Pleasant was a nowadays girl, always up-to-the-minute with good modern ideas, which Miss Petitfour considered a Pleasant change. She knew about cling-free dusting mitts and tornado vacuums, for example, and all the latest cleaning tools.

While the cats appreciated the importance of a good spring clean as much as anyone, they had been rather looking forward instead to spending the morning outside, especially Mustard and Moutarde and Hemdela and Earring, who loved any sort of game that involved madly running around the back garden. And so the cats were not there to witness the crucial moment, when Pleasant – with Miss Petitfour hiding behind the sofa – pulled open the closet door.

I'm sure you can imagine the assortment of items that came hurtling out of the closet when Pleasant opened the door, so I shall only take time to mention a few things: a typewriter, a bicycle with a wicker basket, seashells, a bag of single socks and about a hundred of those small plastic toys that are born out of chocolate eggs, all of which flew out of the closet and pinged every which way. Pleasant had wisely thought to wear her bicycle helmet and goggles, so she was not afraid of flying plastic bits ricocheting off the walls.

Certain words are like twists of crumpled paper jammed into the hole in the bottom of a leaky pail, to keep the story from spilling out too quickly. Words like MEANWHILE, BY THE WAY, IT IS INTERESTING TO NOTE and THAT REMINDS ME OF. Adults use these words all the time when they are afraid things are getting too exciting.

MEANWHILE, on the village green, most of the villagers were busily setting up the Great Spring Jumble Sale. Every five years or so, there was a really massive jumble, a sale of such proportion that it could only be held outside. Out of their cottages the villagers streamed, carrying armloads of rummage – it was almost impossible to believe such quantities could come from such tiny houses. Wagonloads, barrows-full, birdcages-full, hats-full – with pockets bulging, everyone transported their treasures to the green.

Because there was so much to sell, the jumble sale was organised alphabetically. This was the brilliant idea of Mrs Bois-Brioche des Fontana Harridale Quesloe-Brisbane, who had been born

in France and liked to tidy things, and who had volunteered to supervise the massive sale. She firmly believed that the alphabet would keep everything in its place: alarm clocks, bow ties, calculators, collars (dog collars, fur collars, shirt collars) and coriander. Galoshes, gauntlets, goblets. Irons – curling irons, golf irons, waffle irons. Sponges, sponge cake, sponge toffee. Teapots, terrible jokes, tinsel. There were always mistakes made – what were the bunnies doing amid the footballs, frying pans and furbelows, for example? Mrs Bois-Brioche des Fontana Harridale Quesloe-Brisbane was splendid at sorting out these alphabetical catastrophes, for she was very good at the alphabet and never got flustered in the face of jam tarts amid umbrellas, or umbrellas amid jam tarts. Or fossils and fountain pens mixed up with salad bowls and sugar cubes, for that matter.

But Mrs Bois-Brioche des Fontana Harridale Quesloe-Brisbane did have one particular weakness: she always thought people were calling her name. No one could understand why this was so. It would be perfectly understandable if one's name were Mrs Gustavo-Wentworth Worthington Donquist Torresdale Blindon Perstancion-Withers or Mrs Randolfo-Blunt Merritonk Goodland Czerny Attenblock Cardsall-Tentwood, but surely not a name like Bois-Brioche des Fontana Harridale Quesloe-Brisbane. And that is why, while she remained calm in the face of alphabetical chaos, she was also unfortunately prone to nervous fits at jumble sales. Perhaps it was the large crowd, or all that jumble, or her sense of duty that made her think everyone was shouting her name – whatever the reason, she always rushed about, certain she was being called for. But Mrs Bois-Brioche des Fontana Harridale Quesloe-Brisbane was such a jolly sort, and always so generous with the fruit gums in her cardigan pocket, that no one felt grumpy about this small *eccentricity*.

(An *eccentricity* is something everyone has – but everyone has a different one. An *eccentricity* is a quirky thing we like to do just because. Perhaps you always like to put on your right shoe first. Or perhaps you like to count by twos when you're bored. Or perhaps you only like to eat popcorn on Tuesdays. Or perhaps you like to count *digressions* and keep a record of them at the back of every book you read.)

MEANWHILE AGAIN, Miss Petitfour – who all this time had been sitting among the contents of her closet, which had shot out when Pleasant opened the door – suddenly remembered the jumble sale. She had almost forgotten, though the date had been

marked in her calendar for the past five years.
Thinking she might offer for sale her navy-blue peacoat (with buttons with anchors on them), which
was years too short for her, she extracted it from the
pile. But along with the coat, inextricably entangled
with the wire coat hanger, came another wire coat
hanger and another and another, each more tangled
than the next, until a great wire ball, a twisty, jangly
jamboree of metal gibberish, twanged its way out of
the closet. Pleasant Patel felt sure that this tangled,
twangled ball would be a welcome item at the sale

and dragged it across Miss Petitfour's plush living-room carpet into the garden. Miss Petitfour and Pleasant gazed with admiration at this collection of jittery metal glinting in the sunlight.

Now, Minky, Misty, Taffy, Purrsia, Pirate, Mustard, Moutarde, Hemdela, Earring, Grigorovitch, Clasby, Captain Captain, Captain Catkin, Captain Clothespin, Your Shyness and Sizzles were in the garden enjoying a leisurely game of badminton when Miss Petitfour and Pleasant brought out the coat hangers. Immediately, the cats slinked over to inspect the display on the lawn and decided it was a wonderful jungle gym upon which to play.

While the cats were cavorting and climbing, Miss Petitfour and Pleasant, wanting to give the cats a bit of fun, decided to give the coat hangers a good shake. Well, do you think this was wise? To take a ball of gnarly, nervous, knotted wire coat hangers and shake it in the frisky spring breeze? Indeed, no, it was not. What had been simply jangly now became forevermore, eternally, and no-doubts-about-it complicated, snagged and securely snarled.

JUST THEN, with the cats capering among the coat hangers, the breeze turned gusty and the wire tangle began to shiver. The shivering grew deeper and deeper until the whole coat hanger contraption began to shudder as if it would explode. With great presence of mind, Miss Petitfour tied one end of a length of string (she always kept string in her apron pocket in case of emergency) to the nearest coat hanger and tied the other end to her apron. She then grabbed the nearest tablecloth (green gingham for spring) and Pleasant's eager hand, just as the wind picked up.

Off they all sailed!

The cats loved every single one of their flights with Miss Petitfour, but this was perhaps their most exhilarating flight yet. The coat hangers collided and crashed, hummed and thundered, clattered and rumbled. Coat hanger cacophony! With the fresh spring wind rushing through their fur, the cats leaped and swung, hurtling headlong – sixteen cat acrobats on a thrilling coat hanger trapeze.

Luckily, the wind was in the direction of the jumble sale, and along they flew, over Mrs Carruther's

Grocery Shop and Mr Clemmo's Hardware Shop, all the way to the village green. From a distance, it looked as if Miss Petitfour and Pleasant were hanging by a furry, metallic cloud. In fact, the villagers on the green began to panic, thinking that the great rumbling noise they were hearing was thunder. A thunderstorm on the day of the Great Spring Jumble Sale! Disaster!

Just as they reached the far side of the green, the wind suddenly dropped and down Miss Petitfour and Pleasant and the cats clattered – landing like a coat hanger meteorite – right in the middle of the jumble sale. The cats were delighted! In an instant, Minky, Misty, Taffy, Purrsia, Pirate, Mustard, Moutarde, Hemdela, Earring, Grigorovitch, Clasby, Captain Captain, Captain Catkin, Captain Clothespin, Your Shyness and Sizzles were darting with great glee amongst the postage stamps, packets of erasers, moccasins, swimming fins, paint pots and whistles. They ran in and out of the clothes – loose, drab, flouncy, silky, frilly dresses; jackets with zips, clasps, snaps and toggles; trousers that were old-fashioned, new-fangled, shiny, teensy, plain, plaid, too long and too short; hats with feathers, buckles, ribbons and flowers. Cat costume heaven!

The jumble was in an uproar. Everyone was rushing about looking for umbrellas, still thinking it was going to pour rain any minute, or trying to capture the runaway tumbleweed of coat hangers that was rolling through the piles of rummage, collecting things as it went – everything seemed to be in danger of becoming entangled in its wiry grasp. Poor Mrs Bois-Brioche des Fontana Harridale Quesloe-Brisbane was in such a flap; she thought everyone was calling her name at once and ran about not knowing what to do first.

IT IS INTERESTING TO NOTE that Miss Petitfour was still attached to the coat hangers by her apron string, and so she too was running about, hoping to control the haywire menace and perhaps tackle it to a stop.

Working at the jumble sale was poor Colonel By, who had been helping his wife sort through a table full of birdcages, when the coat hangers crashed. Everyone thought of him as *poor* Colonel By because his wife, Mrs Colonel Adria Slope-Nethertop Ashbridge Terrance Poswensky-By, was always giving him a quick wallop with her handbag. Mrs Colonel Adria Slope-Nethertop Ashbridge Terrance Poswensky-By was very sensitive to teasing and always thought her husband was teasing her (though he wasn't). Sometimes she walloped him simply out of affection or when she wanted to get his attention. Some people have habits such as this – they giggle when they're nervous, or they shout when they have nothing to say. Well, the Colonel's wife was a walloper. (I believe we may count this as a *digression*.) In any case, Colonel By and his wife had both been alarmed by the clanging jangle when the coat hangers landed and they can be forgiven for thinking it was raining paper clips. Everyone at the jumble sale was in a muddle, thinking the sky was raining down all sorts of crashing, clashing metal things – nuts and bolts, hubcaps and bottle caps, bin lids and roller skates.

And to top it off, the most outrageous thing of all was that the items at the jumble were now out of alphabetical order! A tuba had smashed into the frisbees, a camera had plunked into the tray of false moustaches – everything had become alphabet soup. Mrs Bois-Brioche des Fontana Harridale Quesloe-Brisbane, realising this, began squealing with distress and chasing after eight hundred marbles as they hurtled towards forty-two rolled-up carpets. Without alphabetical order, who would ever find the soup spoons and the neckties and the false eyelashes and the broken typewriter? The Ps had flipped over into the Qs, the Bs were in the Ds and the Ws had toppled into the Ms!

The jumble sale was in a jumble!

Now, standing in the midst of this bubbling flubdub hubbub, with her hands on her hips, and looking very intelligent, was brave young Pleasant Patel. She was not standing idly by. Oh no, indeed. Pleasant was staring hard at the table full of birdcages. What miraculous thing, she wondered, could a person do with fifty empty birdcages?

Then Pleasant looked across the green and saw two things: the wire ball careening wildly towards her, and all sixteen cats madly waving their tails at her as if they were throwing sixteen footballs. And in a flash, Pleasant had a plan.

When a huge ball is hurtling in your direction at high speed, what do you do? You build a net to catch the goal! Pleasant leaped into action, piling the birdcages one on top of the other. Colonel By – standing by – quickly understood what Pleasant was up to, and he rushed to join in. And just as they finished stacking the very last birdcage at the very tip of the top, the massive coat-hanger ball slammed into

the goal. 'Score!' shouted Colonel By. 'Goal!' cheered Pleasant, waving her arms excitedly, while the cats all caterwauled, 'One to nothing!'

Well, the sound of the goal was near deafening. Everyone on the village green came to a standstill. All eyes turned to the twangling ball and the mound of birdcages. Other than the panting sound of Miss Petitfour, who was still attached to the coat hangers and catching her breath, the village green was absolutely silent.

Rummage was everywhere and every which way, dangling from the trees and gently floating over the grass. And then, during that very moment of absolute, complete and utter silence, a bird – a chiff-chaff warbler – landed on the toppermost birdcage and began to sing.

For a minute, nothing else happened. And then, Mrs Bois-Brioche des Fontana Harridale Quesloe-Brisbane and Mrs

Colonel Adria Slope-Nethertop Ashbridge Terrance Poswensky-By and Mrs Gustavo-Wentworth Worthington Donquist Torresdale Blindon Perstancion-Withers and Mrs Randolfo-Blunt Merritonk Goodland Czerny Attenblock Cardsall-Tentwood and everyone else began to giggle. Then everyone began to laugh so hard they had to sit down, and since everyone was now sitting down, they decided to have a picnic, right then and there, amid the jumble. The cakes from the bake-sale table were passed around, and the little bird who sang at just the right moment hopped about, enjoying the crumbs.

Sometimes things work out differently to how you expect, and sometimes that's when the best things happen. And sometimes a jumble straightens everything out in the end.

Soon, the cats felt a shift in the wind through their fur and they leaped back on to the tagled jamboree of twangling wire coat hangers. All were quickly borne aloft. 'Homeward-ho!' shouted Miss Petitfour, with Pleasant in hand, and feeling very jolly and only a little sorry that she had not had the chance to sell her peacoat.

As always after an airborne adventure, Miss Petitfour set out a magnificent feast. There was currant toast squishy with butter, caramel-marshmallow squares, strawberry boats oozing custard, chocolate eclairs that exploded with cream when the cats bit into them with their little white teeth and − a special treat for Pleasant − a pie made from thick slices of Bramley apple, with just the right amount of tangy in the tangy-sweet.

There was a satisfying silence as all tucked in to the generous tea. Sometimes there was an 'mmm' and a 'yum' and the tiny sound of whiskers being licked clean, but mostly the only sound was the soothing clicketing of metal coat hangers as the giant ball rolled lazily in the breeze, from one end of the garden to THE END.

MISS PETITFOUR

and the

PENNY BLACK

I t was a snow-quiet day, with drifts across the windows and blue light through the frosted panes. With all her cats snoozing peacefully around her in a furry pile-up, Miss Petitfour sat at her work table looking through a large velvet album containing her collection of rare, and not so rare, stamps. She had a fine collection that used to belong to her father. She had stamps with pictures of Peruvian llamas, Indian dragonflies and Mongolian yaks. Stamps with pictures of palm trees and waterbirds, aeroplanes and trains, monarchs and monarchs (insects and kings).

Sometimes stamp makers make mistakes, and stamps with mistakes are the rarest of all. There's the Treskilling Yellow, a stamp that was printed the wrong colour and of which there is only a single one left in the entire world. Or the Inverted Swan, where the picture was printed upside down so it looks as if the swan is swimming in the sky, or the Mauritius Post Office Error, where the words are wrong. Miss Petitfour didn't have any of these rarest of rare stamps in her collection, but she did have a stamp that she treasured most of all – her father's pride and joy: the famous Penny Black. The Penny Black was the very first sticky stamp ever made and has a lovely little picture of Queen Victoria wearing her crown, with her hair pulled back in what looks like a ponytail. Imagine a queen with a ponytail!

Miss Petitfour loved the little pictures, each in its own serrated frame and each seeming to tell its own little story. On snowy days especially, she liked to spread the collection across her lap and dream of travelling to all the places the stamps were from: Tonga and Tunisia, Gibraltar and Jersey, Belgium

and Burma, the Pitcairn and Paracel Islands. Sometimes she gathered the cats, Minky, Misty, Taffy, Purrsia, Pirate, Mustard, Moutarde, Hemdela, Earring, Grigorovitch, Clasby, Captain Captain, Captain Catkin, Captain Clothespin, Your Shyness and Sizzles, and told them stories she made up about these places, stories full of rolling waves and motorcades, damp caves and last-minute saves, musketeers and mountaineers.

Pirate was especially fond of these snowy, stamp-and-story, slumbery afternoons and liked to doze right on top of the open album, his black and white paws hanging over the edge. One afternoon, no one noticed that a stamp had stuck to one of his paws, and when Miss Petitfour closed the velvet album the

Penny Black – worth a small fortune – was no longer among its pages!

The black stamp looked, at a glance, just like a little spot of black fur on Pirate's paw, until Miss Petitfour put on her glasses to read a little poetry before supper time. Then, while she was memorising a poem and gazing at her cats lovingly, her eyes caught sight of the stamp sticking to Pirate's left forepaw. She lunged for the stamp and startled Pirate, who leaped to the top of the bookcase and, in doing so, unstuck the stamp, which flew up and was caught by the breeze at the half-open window.

(Miss Petitfour always left the windows open a little on wintry days, as she loved the smell of snow.) Out flew the Penny Black! And up jumped Miss Petitfour, who grabbed her warmest sweater and her fluffiest muff and pulled the frosty white tablecloth off her table. Clutching the corners, she gusted up to follow the stamp that was, by now, floating rather swiftly on the wind towards the village. The cats, who never missed an opportunity to fly, leaped into formation, linking tails and toes, and up drifted the furry cat-rope, dark and wavering against the white winter sky.

Oh, how the cats loved the ticklish feel of the snowflakes on their fur!

Some words wait to ambush a story right in the middle; they hide until just the right moment, then leap out of nowhere and scare the story into an entirely different direction. Words like TIDAL WAVE, HURRICANE, VOLCANO and EARTHQUAKE. Then there are other words that save the day, words like FORTUNATELY, THANK GOODNESS and WHATEVER WOULD WE HAVE DONE IF YOU

HADN'T REMEMBERED TO BRING THE GLUE. But, FORTUNATELY, there are no natural disasters in this story, and so we can simply continue. (And yes, in case you are counting them, this is a *digression*.)

The Penny Black soared over the houses and fields on its way to town, Miss Petitfour and her cats in close pursuit. The stamp twirled and drifted, ascended and descended, danced and whirled in the snowy gusts. Several times, Miss Petitfour reached out her hand and almost caught it, only to have a fresh gust push the stamp just out of reach.

By this time, the cat-rope was swinging over Mr Patel's Bakery. Just as they were passing over, the stamp shuddered and hovered and then, ever so slowly, so slow it almost seemed to be standing still, the stamp touched down lightly on the corner of the chimney. Miss Petitfour expertly adjusted her table-cloth, and she, along with Minky, Misty, Taffy, Purrsia, Pirate, Mustard, Moutarde, Hemdela, Earring, Grigorovitch, Clasby, Captain Captain, Captain Catkin, Captain Clothespin, Your Shyness and Sizzles, began to descend towards the roof. The moment they landed, in a rather – I'm afraid it must be said – clumsy cat-heap, the corner of the stamp lifted and again the Penny Black floated off. In an instant, Miss Petitfour let out the cloth and once more they took to the breeze, following in mad pursuit and never quite catching up. They raced in circles across the sky like the long black hand of a clock gone berserk. Then, suddenly, the Penny Black halted in mid-air, wavered and lilted, and slowly and finally came to rest at the very tip-top of Mr Clemmo's flagpole, a shiny silver knob that glinted in the late-afternoon, sparkling, snow-filled light.

Oh dear, what was Miss Petitfour to do? All the cats held their small cat breaths, not wanting to stir the stamp, which was balancing in the most fluttery sort of way and would surely jump off if they came near.

THANK GOODNESS Mr Clemmo noticed Miss Petitfour's bright white tablecloth puffed up above his shop (which at first he mistook for the full moon), and he rushed to Miss Petitfour's aid. He quickly urged her to land and, once Miss Petitfour and her cats were all safely on the ground, he brought out a heavy wooden bellows from his shop (the kind of bellows used to stoke the engine of a steam train) and heaved and hawed, creaked and wheezed, blew and bellowed, trying to air-blast the little Penny Black from its perch.

No one in the village had ever heard such shouting and wheezing, caterwauling and hollering. Everyone ran into the street to see what was happening. Children, as we all know, are much quicker than adults to grasp just what to do at a time like this, and immediately they ran back indoors for their butterfly

nets. Then they gathered at the bottom of the flag-pole, waiting for the moment the Penny Black would be dislodged and float to the ground.

Meanwhile, Pirate – who felt responsible for all the mayhem – batted, with his little black and white paws, ever so slightly, the rope that hung loosely up the flagpole, and that little cat-vibration was just what was needed to urge the Penny Black back into the air. All the commotion came to a standstill, and all heads turned upwards to watch as the stamp weaved and wobbled, wafted and wiggled its way lazily down, a little black speck amid the falling snowflakes, straight into the upturned and awaiting butterfly net of Mr Clemmo's niece, Clemmie, who deftly retrieved the stamp from the net and placed it in Miss Petitfour's anxious, outstretched hand.

The crowd erupted into the loudest hurrahs and shouts of congratulations ever heard in the village. All the children ran about in the snow, and Mrs Carruther invited everyone over to her shop for free jelly beans.

The Penny Black was saved!

And for ever after, on snowy days when Miss Petitfour spreads the velvet album across her lap and tells her cats all the made-up stories about all the places the stamps are from, there is now quite another stamp story to tell – all of it absolutely true, from the very quiet beginning to the very loud END.

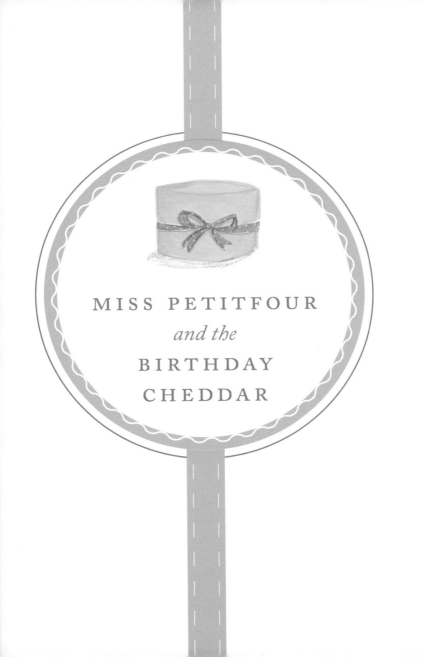

MISS PETITFOUR

and the

BIRTHDAY
CHEDDAR

Miss Petitfour's snow-pawed cat, Minky, loved cheese. She adored cheese, flirted with it, danced with it and brought it lovely presents, like pretty pebbles from the garden, before devouring it with her little Minky teeth. When Miss Petitfour made a fancy salad, Minky watched the way the lettuce leaves bent under the slight weight of the Parmesan; when Miss Petitfour had cheese on toast for tea, Minky noticed how the cheddar melted into every little crevice and crater of the toast. She licked her whiskers greedily when Miss Petitfour lowered her hand to feed her snippets and smidgens, pinches and wedges, slices and crumbs. Minky loved all cheese – Swiss cheese, Edam cheese, Gruyère and Roquefort, Brie cheese and blue cheese, mozzarella and Parmesan, hard cheese, crumbly cheese, creamy cheese, lumpy cheese. Minky even had a cheese calendar that she slept with, which Miss Petitfour had given to her for Christmas. Each month there was a big picture of a different kind of cheese in a mouthwatering pose: blue cheese cavorting with pears, cheddar laughing with apples, Gruyère lounging with grapes, Edam joking with parsley.

Well, it was Minky's birthday, and there was no doubt what her present should be: a huge wheel of extra-extra-extra-old cheddar that would take Minky at least a month to eat. Cheese paradise!

This was a special week, since there was the occasion of Minky's birthday party to look forward to. But, in fact, every week was fun with Miss Petitfour, who followed a strict schedule of fun and more fun. For example, on Tuesdays, Miss Petitfour and the cats took dance instruction with their young friend Pleasant Patel at the Twirl-About School of Dance (their sign was an enormous tap shoe), where they learned every sort of step ever invented: ballet, tango, waltz, samba, gavotte, Scottish reel, bunny hop, hip hop, foxtrot. Bourrée and bergamask, bossa nova and bolero. Brando, buck-and-wing, conga and cotillion.

Now, hold on a moment, I know what you're thinking: why would anyone want to know the steps to all these dances? Well, suppose one day you are sitting next to a billionaire on a bus and he turns to you and says: 'If you can name me twenty dances I've never heard of, I'll give you a shiny new coin.' Then you'll be glad you read this long list of dances, won't you? And Miss Petitfour and Pleasant also thought there might just come a day when all the prancing and twirling would come in handy.

Where were we? Oh yes: the hula, the hornpipe, the hambo, the fandango and farandole. Limbo, kolo, mambo and mazurka. Minuet, merengue, moresca and polka. Rigaudon, roundel, salterello, strathspey. And Miss Petitfour's very favourites – the tarantella and the tricotee.

On Thursdays, Mrs Collarwaller closed her bookshop early and brought over her *Big Book of Ballads*, a heavy leather volume with gold embossing, which took both her arms to carry, and also her *Pocket Book of Sea Shanties*, which was only the size of her hand but was as thick as ten cheese sandwiches. They sat together at Miss Petitfour's piano, learning old songs – each with twenty-five verses – about girls dressing as boys to stow away on ships, and talking blackbirds, and fish hooks and watery brooks, and *spickit* and *sparkit* snakes – that is to say, snakes that are speckled and spotted. They also learned songs full of impossible tasks – oceans emptied using only a soup spoon, and shirts sewn without any thread – and everyone a-sailing and a-roving all over the briny deep. They sang, 'heigh-ho laddie-o' and 'the waves

may roll and the winds may blow' and, afterwards, they flopped down on Miss Petitfour's sofa, exhausted by all their boisterous chorusing and plank-walking and perilous pirate voyages.

And on Fridays, Miss Petitfour went shopping, an outing all her cats loved, and they would wait patiently in the garden for lift-off. Minky, Misty, Taffy, Purrsia, Pirate, Mustard, Moutarde, Hemdela, Earring, Grigorovitch, Clasby, Captain Captain, Captain Catkin, Captain Clothespin, Your Shyness and Sizzles wrapped themselves one to another and off they went. And on this particular Friday, they were on a special mission to buy Minky's birthday cheddar and other party favours, and the big paisley tablecloth puffed full, like the cheeks of a birthday girl ready to blow out the candles.

Some words are like a hailstorm during the middle of a picnic, or a flat tyre on a lovely journey, or a fallen tree across a path, and these words stop a story immediately and swivel it off in another direction entirely. Words like BUT, HOWEVER, IF ONLY, SADLY and UNFORTUNATELY.

UNFORTUNATELY, the wind was blowing in the wrong direction. Instead of taking Miss Petitfour and Minky, Misty, Taffy, Purrsia, Pirate, Mustard, Moutarde, Hemdela, Earring, Grigorovitch, Clasby, Captain Captain, Captain Catkin, Captain Clothespin, Your Shyness and Sizzles in the direction of the Party Whatnot Shop (their sign was a gargantuan party hat) – where Miss Petitfour was hoping to buy all the birthday treats, including balloons and banners and icing sugar and ice cream and of course the great wheel of cheese – the wind blew them in the direction of the river, where, as we all know, there are no handy shops whatsoever. Moreover, the water was terribly cold, as it came directly from the mountaintop, and furthermore, the cats did not like to wet their whiskers, unless of course it was in vats of cream.

Sizzles' tail dangled dangerously close to the brisk current. All the cats were scrambling upwards, towards Miss Petitfour's basket, as they all sank lower and lower, barely avoiding plunging into the rapids.

What was Miss Petitfour to do?

The wind drew them lower and then just a bit

higher again, and lower and higher, as if they were on an invisible swing. Clasby nearly lost his bobble hat in the waves, and Your Shyness's lace collar got a soaking from some passing spray. On and on, further and further down the river, they dipped and rose.

Some words are like rays of light, white knights or a safety pin at the right moment, and these words are as useful as sticky tape just when the page has ripped, fixing a story in an instant. Words like UNBELIEVABLY, BY GREAT GOOD FORTUNE and BY CHANCE.

BY CHANCE and UNBELIEVABLY and BY GREAT GOOD FORTUNE, Mr Coneybeare happened to be out in his sailboat, enjoying the stiff breeze on the river, with his cloud identification book (identifying clouds was one of his hobbies), when he noticed a shadowy shape hopping low across the water. He could not identify the kind of cloud that could make such a shadow – certainly not a *stratus* cloud or a *cirrus* or a *cumulonimbus*. Was it the treacherous *waterspout*? For a moment, he even thought he had discovered a new kind of cloud and became very excited. Perhaps, he thought, it could be named after its discoverer – the 'Coneybeare cloud'! (As we know, the cats had once before been mistaken for a cloud, on the day of the jumble, and so Mr Coneybeare can be easily forgiven for being confused.)

MEANWHILE, while Mr Coneybeare was thinking these cloudy thoughts (which we might almost consider to be a *digression*), Miss Petitfour and the cats were trying to think of ways to save themselves from a dousing. There were no convenient trees to swing their way to and no handy fishermen with nets to scoop them from danger.

As you no doubt know, Miss Petitfour was an excellent pilot, and she understood air currents and wind velocity. She deduced that if they worked with the wind, instead of against it, perhaps they could make their escape. Now, do you think it is wise to work with the wind instead of against it? Yes, it is! And, by now, Miss Petitfour had spotted the tiny white speck of Mr Coneybeare's sail further down the river and knew if they all worked together and swung even harder, they might propel themselves as far as his little boat. So, with a brief instruction to her cats, and the captain cats mewing captain-y

commands, they began to throw themselves first in one direction then another, wildly swinging like the pendulum of a grandfather clock.

All was going very well until Mustard and Moutarde got confused and went one way instead of the other. All the cats collided in a bang-up snarly mess. They were just about to plummet into the water, when suddenly, all those Tuesday afternoons of twirling finally came in useful. 'Waltz!' commanded Miss Petitfour. And the cats quickly obeyed, waltzing in perfect unison above the rushing river. Expertly, they swayed through the air, never missing a step, and in another moment, they were safely out of danger.

By now, Mr Coneybeare had realised he was not seeing a *waterspout*, for *waterspouts* do not waltz. He recognised the familiar furry cat-rope and wondered if the capable Miss Petitfour might welcome the use of his sailboat. Swiftly, he steered his sail in the direction of their tails. Miss Petitfour's navigation was perfect and, at exactly the right moment – for it really wouldn't do for Miss Petitfour to fly past Mr Coneybeare's little boat and miss it entirely –

Mr Coneybeare tossed a rope high into the air, the way someone might throw confetti at a wedding, and Sizzles, in mid-waltz, caught the end of the rope expertly with his tail. Then, in a graceful fall of fur, all the cats primly plopped on to the deck. At the same time, Miss Petitfour nimbly gathered in her tablecloth and landed on the pillow right next to Mr Coneybeare, who, with a bashful smile, said how very pleased he was that she was able to plop by.

Both wild and mild adventures are made for the pleasure of returning home, and after a stop at the shop for a packet of fake moustaches, a box of chocolate buttons, sugar doughnuts, spumoni, catnip and party-favour whatnots, and of course a huge wheel of birthday cheddar, Miss Petitfour, Minky, Misty, Taffy, Purrsia, Pirate, Mustard, Moutarde, Hemdela, Earring, Grigorovitch, Clasby, Captain Captain, Captain Catkin, Captain Clothespin, Your Shyness and Sizzles all piled into Mr Coneybeare's red sports car and were home in no time at all. A huge birthday tea was prepared, including Minky's favourite two-layer birthday cheddar-cake. Doubly-round cheese paradise!

Minky would always remember this birthday as the best one of all. Not everyone is lucky enough to mark their birthday with an almost-dunking, a ripping river rescue, and a ride in a sailboat and a sports car all in a single afternoon. After tea, everyone snoozed in the garden on the very same paisley tablecloth that Miss Petitfour had tied up at the corners, and that had carried them from the beginning of their very rousing adventure to its very sleepy END.

MISS PETITFOUR

and the
'OOM'

It was an autumn day, with exciting weather – shivering blasts of wind and silver clouds against a purple sky. This was Miss Petitfour's favourite kind of day and her favourite season, when it's cold enough to wear a cardigan and blustery enough for thrilling sails across the countryside. Chilly days gave Miss Petitfour extra energy, and today she was eager to gather the cats and her most colourful tablecloth and sail off on an adventure.

The cats loved autumn too. They liked to make tottering mountains of leaves, so high that the slightest breath of a breeze would tremble the pile. The three captains – Captain Captain, Captain Catkin and Captain Clothespin – and Pirate liked to sneak their way (very carefully!) into the bottom of these shifting, shuddering mountains, and there, curled up in their secret, crinkly spot, they would listen to the whole whispery weight of leaves stirring above them. They hid there quietly, with little corners of light peeking in through the leaves.

The captain cats and Pirate loved everything to do with wind and boats and the sea. They loved fancy sailor's knots and the shiny buttons on a captain's uniform and buccaneers' big brass belt buckles. And so, as the leaf mountain heaved and crackled, they would close their eyes and pretend they were on a big wooden sailing ship – you know the kind, with billowing square sails and ropes snapping against the mast. Pirate and the captains loved sea stories, but weren't too keen about actually going on a

voyage, which might require, at some point, getting wet. So, they were very content just to curl up and listen to the wind and dream of the sea. A simply splendid way to spend a morning!

While Pirate and the captains imagined sea voyages inside the leaf mountain, the other cats ran in circles, gathering more and more leaves on to the pile. They jumped to catch falling leaves, tackling them in mid-air. Taffy was especially good at the flying tackle, bringing down more leaves himself than all the other cats together. Tackling leaves before they reach the ground is not as easy as it sounds. In fact, if you've ever tried, you know that you can leap for an entire afternoon and not catch a single one! But the cats knew a secret: you must throw yourself into the air all the places where the leaf is not. You must jump sideways, away from the direction the leaf seems to be falling in – and then, when the wind changes its mind at the very last second, you will be there to catch it.

And so, on this particular October morning, when Miss Petitfour looked out of her kitchen window, she saw all the cats in squirming sideways leaps – long furry cat-blurs in the air – while gentle gusts blew the leaves every which way. The wind was so full of cats and colours that Miss Petitfour decided right then and there to bake buttery leaf-shaped biscuits, with orange and yellow and red icing, for the cats' tea. And leaf biscuits never require jumping in the opposite direction. On the contrary, they always sit quietly on the plate just waiting to be caught and never jump away from your fingers at the last second. And that's why we never get tired of eating leaf biscuits and can gobble up quite a few before needing to take a rest.

While Miss Petitfour sieved powdery flour, making clouds of white dust and speckling the counter, and while she scooped sugar and made little bowlfuls of icing, she thought about the Great Annual Festival of *Festooning* that was to take place that afternoon.

The Festival of *Festooning* always attracted a big crowd, including many people who came by mistake, thinking it wasn't about *festooning*, but about cartooning or ballooning. *Festooning* is, of course, just a fancy word for cleverly decorating things, for draping ribbons and streamers and lace and jewels on things to dress them up. A perfect example is decorating a Christmas tree, *festooning* it with strings of popcorn and shiny garlands. Fancy occasions can always use some *festooning* and everyone *festoons* in their own way: mechanics hang shiny new nuts and bolts as ornaments, chefs hang gleaming spoons and icicles of twisted aluminium foil, and office assistants make extra-long streamers out of Post-it notes and paper clips.

As you well know, the cats were especially fond of *festooning* themselves – with velvet and satin ribbon, and skeins of wool, and necklaces from Miss Petitfour's costume jewellery box. The cats also liked to use themselves and each other to *festoon* furniture and to join their tails and dangle from curtains and curl around the banister. They would create an elaborate and dramatic display of themselves, and Miss Petitfour would take their photograph. Say cheese!

Miss Petitfour was very proud of her cats and was looking forward to the great display they were going to present at the festival, hoping to win the shiny silver trophy for first prize.

While she was baking her leaf biscuits and daydreaming about the festival, Miss Petitfour's mind began to wander to other interesting topics. (*Digression* alert!)

Miss Petitfour thought about the fact that there are some things you have to do every day – like brush your teeth and put on shoes and eat breakfast. Some people believe that if you have to do the same old dull thing every day, then you should just try to ignore it as much as you can and hope it will go away. Or that you should rush through whatever it is at top speed, so you won't have time to be bored. But Miss Petitfour believed that if you had to do something every day, then that was all the more reason to make it fun. What do you think? Is it better to hold your nose and slowly eat little crumbs of cauliflower, or is it better to steam the whole thing and serve it on a big platter like a giant snowball? Is it better to brush your teeth wearily, as if you were running out of batteries, or to brush your teeth singing long verses of sea shanties in your head and stamping your foot to the rhythm? You know sea shanties, those long songs with lots of verses that Miss Petitfour and Mrs Collarwaller sang on Thursdays and that sailors sing while they do what sailors do, which is mostly a lot of pulling hard on ropes – to let down the anchor and pull it back up again, or to lower those big sails and raise them back up again. Well, Miss Petitfour was all for a good sea shanty while brushing her teeth, pulling that toothbrush up and down and stamping her little foot:

Were you ever in Quebec,
bonny laddie, highland laddie,
stowing timber on the deck,
bonny highland laddie!
Hey ho and away we go,
bonny highland laddie!

Of course, the captain cats always joined in, thumping their tails to the beat.

And, as far as eating breakfast every day was concerned, Miss Petitfour was definitely of the same school of thought. If you have to sit at the table and pretend to be hungry, just because you-probably-will-be-hungry-the-moment-you-get-to-school-so-you'd-better-eat-something-before-you-leave, then you might as well make your French toast in different shapes and build a house out of it, or cut your grapefruit into circles to look like the sun.

Miss Petitfour thought ordinary things should be made grand – or, in the case of Minky, who was the smallest of all the cats, 'little grand'. (Tiny Minky was a slip-through-a-keyhole kind of cat, who was scared of whole carrots the size of baseball bats and apples as big as pumpkins – for that is how big they looked to her. So, Miss Petitfour cut her carrots into little swords and sliced her apples into little round shields, just the perfect size for Viking Minky!)

While she was baking her leaf biscuits, Miss Petitfour also thought about the fact that there were certain tiresome things people were always saying like, 'Go on now, eat it all up, it's good for you.' If people really insist on saying such dreary things, then we may as well hear them as if they were fun. For example, the next time someone says, 'It's good for you,' then you should simply hear, 'Good for *you*!' the way someone says it after you've done something incredible, like reciting the alphabet backwards or painting a picture of a capybara. 'Good for *you*! Good for *you*!' Or when someone says, 'Hurry up then, are you going to take all day?' you should just hear, 'Take all day!' and not feel rushed at all.

These are the sorts of things that Miss Petitfour thought about, and so she was never bored. Even when there's nothing else to do, there's always something to think about! You can think about cats who play badminton, or confetti kings who chase clouds, or, if you're like Minky, you can think about . . . cheese.

Now, Miss Petitfour had just put the leaf biscuits into the oven to bake – in fact, she had just shut the oven door – when she heard a peculiar noise. It was a very faint *whump* of a sound, coming from quite a distance away. It sounded as if a feather pillow had exploded. Just a single, faint puff of air – like an 'oompah' without the 'pah', or a 'boom' without the 'b'.

For a long moment, Miss Petitfour stood in the kitchen and listened. But, as everything was just as peaceful after the 'oom' as it had been before, she decided to think no more about it. And, just as soon as the leaf biscuits were baked and put on a platter to cool, she and the cats readied themselves to fly off to the festival.

Oh, it was the perfect day for flying! Far below, they saw the countryside all golden and bronze, all the trees shining their autumn colours. The wind made the long grasses swim in the fields, and Miss Petitfour and the cats looked down with joyful hearts. The beauty of the day made each of the cats, and even Miss Petitfour, mew with pleasure. Young Clasby mewed the loudest, for he especially loved the trees and fields from above and always looked carefully, so later he could paint a picture of what he saw.

The flight was glorious – and fast too. In ten minutes flat, they had sped far past the outskirts of the village and beyond to the Exhibition Hall, which was already filling up with *festooners*.

There was such a bustling! Everyone seemed to be running around pell-mell, carrying bolts of rustling stiff crêpe paper and spools of silent velvet ribbon; there was the swish of tinsel and the jittering of plastic beads. And everyone had brought such fancy objects to *festoon*! Castles and bridges and giant towers, stuffed giraffes and knights in armour. Miss Petitfour and the cats stared in amazement. And throughout the crowd, weaving to and fro, clutching a clipboard and a magnifying glass, was Padmé Patel (Pleasant's grandmother), who was the official judge of the competition and who was having a good look around while everyone was setting up.

Miss Petitfour stood back and let the cats get to work. While all around them *festooners* were struggling with bulky castles and heavy trellises, the cats had brought with them only a single extra-long strand of gold ribbon. Elegantly, and with perfect teamwork, the cats slipped this way and that and, in no time at all, had pulled the ribbon into a perfect cat's cradle. You know the game of cat's cradle, when you wrap string around your hands and pass the cradle from one person to the next? You don't? Ask someone immediately! We'll wait here.

All right, does everyone now know what the game of cat's cradle is? Fine. The cats' plan was simple: they would *festoon* themselves with the ever-changing cat's cradle, in a series of delightful poses. A sure winner!

They were just settling down, waiting for the contest to begin, when Miss Petitfour cupped her hand over her ear. She had extremely good hearing and, in the midst of the chatter and bustle of the busy Exhibition Hall, she was sure she'd heard that muffled 'oom' again. It is not every day we hear a mysterious 'oom', let alone two, and Miss Petitfour was now certain something was amiss. She rushed outside.

Miss Petitfour looked up and down and all

around, and then she noticed a patch of sky that seemed to be glittering and shimmering and twisting in the weirdest way. And furthermore, it seemed to be swivelling directly above Mr Coneybeare's confetti factory. Time to investigate! Quickly gathering cats and cloth, Miss Petitfour stretched out her arm to the autumn wind.

Today was Sunday and the factory was closed, but Miss Petitfour knew that Mr Coneybeare was probably inside, as he liked to sit in the quiet of the factory on Sunday afternoons and catch up on his thinking. Mr Coneybeare was very keen to discover new uses for confetti, and every Sunday, he would let his mind wander through the possibilities. Sometimes he would make various experiments, and it so happened that on this very Sunday he had invented his masterpiece: Coneybeare's Super-Sticky Confetti, which stuck to everything it touched. And it was this experiment that had so abruptly ended with the 'oom'.

The shimmering tornado above the confetti factory was growing bigger by the second, and

Miss Petitfour had to be very careful to avoid getting caught in it. They circled to and fro, here and there, trying to find a way through.

SUDDENLY, the wind shifted and Miss Petitfour seized her chance. They slid right down to the ground through the centre of the tornado – it was like swooshing down a tunnel slide – and landed neatly at the front door of the factory. Miss Petitfour found the key under the mat and let herself in, the cats winding excitedly around her feet.

The factory was huge, with two giant glass urns of confetti standing like sentries on either side of the front door. The vast building was completely quiet, and confetti was everywhere. The walls glimmered like the inside of an ice cave, giving off a pale glow. Miss Petitfour could now see that something had gone terribly wrong and that the 'oom' had been a confetti explosion! No one ever wanted the confetti factory to explode of course, yet, over the years, everyone in the village had secretly wondered what would happen if it did. Would confetti shoot through the chimney like a cannon? Would the tiny polka dots make everyone sneeze?

It must have been quite a blast, for everything inside the factory was coated in sparkling paper dust: the desks, the lamps, the telephones, the big confetti-making machines. It looked as if no one had been there for centuries. The cats began to explore, lifting their paws high through drifts of confetti snow, and soon, like Minky, they all seemed to be wearing little shining socks. Miss Petitfour looked down at her own feet and saw that her blue shoes were sparkling.

JUST THEN, a small sound echoed through the factory. It was a yelp, or perhaps 'help', and it was coming from the far end of the building where big silver vats were lined up, ready to fill little round tins with Coneybeare's Confetti: Extra-Shimmery.

Miss Petitfour and the cats heard the voice again. They waded as quickly as they could through the drifts of dots and followed the feeble cry.

Miss Petitfour stood on the tips of her toes and looked over the edge of a vast vat. There, peeking out of the Extra-Shimmery was the very embarrassed face of Mr Coneybeare, who was sunk and afraid to move, for fear he would sink deeper. His face and hair and eyebrows were shining with paper dust, as if he were wearing a mask. Poor Mr Coneybeare! He had spent all morning experimenting, trying to find the perfect recipe for Super-Sticky. But his last batch had blown up, and the confetti explosion had oomed him straight into a vat of Extra-Shimmery.

Without wasting a moment, Miss Petitfour twisted her tablecloth and threw one end towards Mr Coneybeare, who caught it in his teeth like a fish catching a hook. The cats formed a chain, and with Miss Petitfour tugging too, out popped Mr Coneybeare. He was completely shimmery, from the top of his head to the tips of his shoes. And Miss Petitfour and all the cats thought the same thought at exactly the same moment: encased in paper dust – including his hair and eyebrows – Mr Coneybeare looked exactly like a statue!

EXTRA-
SHIMMERY

The thought of statues reminded Miss Petitfour of the *festooning* festival and, afraid the cats would miss the judging, she hurriedly led Mr Coneybeare outside. She readied her tablecloth, linked his arm in hers and, without a moment's pause, up they flew, deftly avoiding the twister of confetti still hovering above the factory. Mr Coneybeare was so astonished to be suddenly in the air that he barely even realised what was happening before they'd already landed and were rushing off to take their places for the judging. During the short flight, the wind had blown away all the paper dust from Mr Coneybeare and, though dazed, he looked his old self again.

What a grand spectacle greeted them in the Exhibition Hall! Everyone was now ready, and such a sight had never been seen! Everything sparkled, shone and gleamed – it was a wonderland of *festooning*. The cats quickly assembled themselves in their assigned place, near a large skylight that was left open to let in the lovely autumn air.

If you've been reading about Miss Petitfour's adventures – and of course you have since you're reading this sentence – then you will know how handy a *coincidence* can be. A *coincidence* is something that happens at just the right moment. Say, for example, just at the very moment you find a pound on the pavement, the ice-cream van stops in front of you. That's a tasty *coincidence*. Or say, just at the very moment your hot cocoa is ready, a marshmallow falls out of an aeroplane and lands in your cup. That's also a tasty *coincidence*. Stories use *coincidences* all the time to fix tricky tangles. You can usually tell when one is coming because, COINCIDENTALLY, the story will use the word COINCIDENTALLY. And similar words such as: IT JUST SO HAPPENED, IMPOSSIBLY or INCREDIBLY. Now, just to make sure all these special words work, let's try them out!

IT JUST SO HAPPENED that the confetti tornado above the factory, consisting of Extra-Shimmery and the very first batch of Super-Sticky, had begun to move. Slowly at first, then picking up speed in the breeze, the swirling confetti began to race across the sky towards the village, and then past the village, towards the outskirts and the Exhibition Hall. And, INCREDIBLY, the confetti ran smack into a cross-breeze that smashed into it with such force that the twister broke apart and cascaded straight down to the ground in a storm of glistening powder. And, IMPOSSIBLY, the exact spot of the collision in the sky was directly above the open skylight of the Exhibition Hall! And INCREDIBLY, IMPOSSIBLY and COINCIDENTALLY, Mr Coneybeare JUST SO HAPPENED to be standing directly beneath the deluge!

In a trice, Mr Coneybeare was a statue once more.

For a single, startled moment, the cats and Miss Petitfour just stood there, blinking with surprise. Then, all at once, Minky, Misty, Taffy, Purrsia, Pirate, Mustard, Moutarde, Hemdela, Earring, Grigorovitch, Clasby, Captain Captain, Captain Catkin, Captain Clothespin, Your Shyness and Sizzles sprang into action. They circled Mr Coneybeare and, all of one mind, the cats turned to Your Shyness, whose glowing fur was as bright and shiny as a gold coin. In a single leap, she jumped on to

Mr Coneybeare's head, where she looked just like a sparkling gold crown.

At that very instant, Judge Patel reached them and was struck by what she thought was an amazingly lifelike statue of the confetti king. 'Why, that's positively extraordinary!' she said. 'I could swear it was Mr Coneybeare himself!' She paused. 'And what a singularly simple *festoon*!' And then she placed the silver trophy in Miss Petitfour's hand.

The crowd went wild. They picked up Mr Coneybeare and carried him out of the door to the garden, where there was to be a huge party to celebrate the winning *festoon*. They deposited him near a fountain, and there he stood, indeed looking just like a fine piece of sculpture.

Shy Mr Coneybeare, the confetti king, was dumbfounded. What with the shock of being exploded into a vat, and airlifted into a *festooning* festival, and being mistaken for a statue, and helping to win first prize for Miss Petitfour and the cats, and being carried off by a cheering crowd, he was completely undone.

Mr Coneybeare began to totter.

Miss Petitfour, who was a very good noticer, saw that the events of the afternoon had been all too much for Mr Coneybeare, who was not used to such excitement, and she thought perhaps a quick getaway was best. So, gathering the cats around her and readying her tablecloth, she held out her hand to Mr Coneybeare for their getaway flight.

Sometimes a story depends on finding something – a key to a secret door, a magic ring, a hidden passageway. Sometimes you have to look down to find it (like your slipper under the bed) and sometimes you have to look up to find it (like a balloon caught in a tree) and sometimes, if you're really lucky, what you're looking for, finds you.

As soon as Mr Coneybeare took Miss Petitfour's hand, his feet began to lift off the ground. And exactly then, he understood: sometimes, all you must do is reach out your hand for something wonderful to happen.

The cats quickly linked themselves and, forming a furry circle with dear Miss Petitfour and the new-to-flight Mr Coneybeare, they all ascended together. Soon the noise of the exhibition grounds grew dim and was far behind them as they flew back towards the village.

Miss Petitfour always thought of the autumn air as 'deliciously' cold, and it was delicious, up in the sky above the village. The kind of cold that makes everything bright and clear. For a long while, Miss Petitfour, Mr Coneybeare and all the cats hovered in the deepening sky. They watched as, one by one, and then by twos and threes, the lights came on in the village.

Cosy Mrs Carruther turned on the reading lamp with the big orange lampshade, next to the sofa where her four children gathered every night for their evening story. She slid the baby's chair next to her, and the other children fell into a heap to listen. Even the baby, who didn't understand a word but loved to hear the sound of his mother's voice, listened the way we all do when we're being read to and we're just about to fall asleep, the words floating in the air. And cosy Mrs Carruther stopped reading for a moment and looked about her at the beautiful faces of her children, each of them eager to find out what would happen next in the story.

Down the street, outside Mrs Collarwaller's shop, the great wooden sign in the shape of a book creaked on its hinges in the wind. Mrs Collarwaller heard the creaking and went to the window to look out at the blustery night. It was very snug looking out from inside. Soon she made a cup of tea and was sitting in the ho-hum half of her warm shop and, almost just as soon, she was having a nap, safe and peaceful as a picture in a book.

Above the bakery, the giant wooden cupcake swung back and forth outside Pleasant Patel's bedroom, where Pleasant was sunk in her favourite beanbag chair reading and, as she always did, eating her late-afternoon baguette, freshly baked and with just the right crunchiness on the outside. If Miss Petitfour and Mr Coneybeare and all the cats hadn't been quite so high up above the village, they might have heard Pleasant Patel's favourite sound – the lovely sound of baguette crunching – as Pleasant turned the pages. She always crunched faster when the story turned exciting, and that evening she was just at the part of the story where the hero hides himself (*crunch*) in a barrel (*crunch*) and rolls himself into the river (*crunch crunch crunch*) in a grand and daring (*crunch crunch crunch crunch crunch*) escape.

A few doors down from Mr Patel's Bakery, Clemmie was teaching her dog how to rip the Velcro open on her running shoes, so she wouldn't have to bend down when she was in a hurry or when her hands were full.

And, almost at the edge of the village, in their house next to the river, Colonel By and his wife were just settling down with a pot of tea to listen to a symphony on the radio, as they always did on a Sunday afternoon. Mrs By gently walloped her husband to make sure he was listening to a particularly beautiful bit, and Colonel By smiled at the thought of how much he might have missed in this world had she not been there to show him.

For a long moment, everyone in the village, and the village itself, with its sounds of crunching, ripping and walloping, and with its swaying signs of cupcakes and books, hammers and tap shoes, and with lamplight in the windows, seemed to be content.

Minky gently brushed Miss Petitfour's cheek with her fluffy tail to remind Miss Petitfour that it was getting dark – which it was – and, well, as everyone knows, when it begins to get dark, it's time to head for home. (It's very difficult to navigate when you can't see where you're going.) Skilfully, Miss Petitfour leaned into the cold October wind and slowly began to gather in her sail. Mr Coneybeare, learning by the minute, had soon got the hang of flying, and together, with the furry streamer of cats, in no time at all, they were making their gentle descent into Miss Petitfour's garden.

It was evening now, and a lovely path of orange light from Miss Petitfour's kitchen window poured out across the lawn. The cats jumped up on to the window sill, and they all peeked in. They saw that the table was laid out, just as Miss Petitfour had left it all those hours ago, before the excitement of the afternoon, all set and waiting there, as if it hadn't been the most astoundingly thrilling day, with the platter of leaf biscuits still sitting calmly in the centre of the table. And all the cats – littlest Minky and Misty and Taffy and Purrsia and Pirate and Mustard and Moutarde and Hemdela and Earring and Grigorovitch and Clasby and Captain Captain and Captain Catkin and Captain Clothes-pin and Your Shyness and, the longest cat of all, Sizzles – licked their lips at exactly the same moment and crowded around Miss Petitfour's ankles, looking up at her. And, with everyone gazing at her – Mr Coneybeare smiling, and the cats all mewing – with everyone around her very happy and suddenly very hungry, Miss Petitfour gathered her tablecloth, stretched out her arm and opened the door.

It was good to be home.

The fire was soon lit, the kettle was soon whistling, and everyone sat around the table – or on the table or under the table – and Miss Petitfour and Mr Coneybeare and Minky warmed their toes contentedly in their stocking feet. There would be many wonderful adventures to look forward to, once the treats had all been devoured, adventures of just the right size, as wonderful as that very day, from its leafy beginning to its leaf-biscuit END.

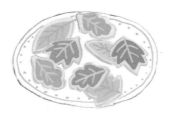

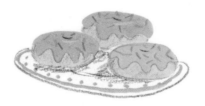

ACKNOWLEDGEMENTS

Prodigious thanks to Tara Walker for her *acuity*, kindness and care,

to Ellen Seligman and Liz Calder for embracing this book from the start,

to Emma Block, for bringing Miss Petitfour's world to the page,

to copyeditor Jennifer Stokes and designer Kelly Hill for precision and *panache*,

to Eve, David and Viva for joyful *camaraderie*.

A lifelong thanks to Janis and Rosie Bellow and the whole wonderful Freedman family.

And above all to Rebecca and Evan . . . for everything and always . . .

ANNE MICHAELS is the internationally award-winning author of *Fugitive Pieces*, which was made into a feature film, and *The Winter Vault*, as well as several volumes of poetry. Her work has appeared in translation in over forty countries around the world. *The Adventures of Miss Petitfour* is her first book for children.

EMMA BLOCK is the illustrator of *Tea and Cake* and several books for children. She has worked with clients including Anthropologie, Uniqlo and Hallmark. Emma likes charity shops, tea and very sharp pencils. Visit her online at emmablock.co.uk.